What Goes Up in Flight?

written by Pam Holden

1

Look at the bees. They are flying high.

bees

Look at the birds. They are flying high.

4

birds

Look at all the flags.
They are flying high.

flags

Look at all the kites. They are flying high.

kites

9

Look at the balloons.
They are flying high.

Look at all the planes.
They are flying high.

planes

13

Look at the helicopters.
They are flying high.

helicopters

15

Look at the rocket. It is flying very high!